Dear Parents:

Children learn to read in stages, and all children develop reading skills at different ages. **Ready Readers**™ were created to promote children's interest in reading and to increase their reading skills. **Ready Readers**™ are written on two levels to accommodate children ranging in age from three through eight. These stages are meant to be used only as a guide.

Stage 1: Preschool-Grade 1
Stage 1 books are written in very short, simple sentences with large type. They are perfect for children who are getting ready to read or are just becoming familiar with reading on their own.

Stage 2: Grades 1-3
Stage 2 books have longer sentences and are a bit more complex. They are suitable for children who are able to read but still may need help.

All the **Ready Readers**™ tell varied, easy-to-follow stories and are colorfully illustrated. Reading will be fun, and soon your child will not only be ready, but eager to read.

STAGE 1 Ready Readers™ Preschool-Grade 1

FREDDIE'S BIRTHDAY SURPRISE

Written by Eugene Bradley Coco
Illustrated by Susan Marino

Modern Publishing
A Division of Unisystems, Inc.
New York, New York 10022

Today is a special day.
Today is Freddie's birthday.

Freddie dresses quickly.

Then he runs downstairs.

"I wonder what presents I will get for my birthday?" says Freddie.

"Hi, Mom. Hi, Dad."

"Hi, Freddie."

"Where did they hide my presents?"
Freddie says.

Freddie looks in the den.

No presents there.

Freddie looks in the playroom.
No presents there.

Freddie even looks behind
the big clock in the hall.
No presents there, either.

No presents anywhere.

"There must be presents
somewhere," says Freddie.

Freddie runs to Bobby's house.

"Bobby will have a present for me."

Bobby isn't home.

Freddie runs to Annie's house.

"Annie will have a present for me."

Annie isn't home, either.

No one is home. Freddie is sad.

"Everyone forgot my birthday,"
he says.

"Come home, Freddie," calls his mother.
"It's time for lunch."

Freddie walks in the door.

"Surprise! Happy birthday, Freddie!"

There is cake. There is candy.

There are games to play.

There are presents.

One from Mom. One from Dad.

One from Bobby. One from Annie.

Freddie is happy.

What a great birthday surprise.

Happy birthday, Freddie.